45253

D1080112

SECRETS
СИКРЭТС

ALICE McLERRAN

LOTHROP, LEE & SHEPARD BOOKS

NEW YORK

First Edition 1 2 3 4 5 6 7 8 9 10

Library of Congress Cataloging in Publication Data
McLerran, Alice. Secrets / by Alice McLerran.
p.   cm. Summary: Mark is not looking forward to spending eight afternoons taking his little sister to play with her Russian friend but his friend Jeff persuades him that this will be a good opportunity for some counterespionage. ISBN 0-688-09545-3 [1. Prejudices—Fiction. 2. Russians—Fiction. 3. Friendship—Fiction.] I. Title. PZ7.M47872 Se 1990 [Fic]—dc20

90-30915 CIP AC

ТУ АЛ МАЙ СОВЕТ ФРЭНДЗ

AUTHOR'S NOTE

While the characters in this story of course do not have counterparts in reality, no author conjures up a tale from thin air. I would be ungrateful if I did not state that into the Russian family pictured here is woven some of the warmth, wisdom, and kindness of many Soviet friends I first knew at Fermi National Accelerator Laboratory.

There are certain difficulties in writing a tale of a Soviet-American friendship at a time when relations between the United States and the Soviet Union are changing rapidly. As this book goes to press, the Soviet Union is undergoing transformations so dramatic that the circumstances sketched in this story will almost certainly soon be history. The uncertainties—and the hopes—of one particular moment in time however, shape only the setting of this story. Its core deals with issues less vulnerable to change. Questions of trust and doubt, of caring and letting go, will continue to matter in whatever futures lie around the bend.

1

"But how can you really be sure they aren't spies?" Jeff's eyes were on the basketball hoop as he spoke. Then with easy grace he ran forward, leaped, and sent the ball neatly in.

Mark moved under the net to catch the ball and absentmindedly tossed it back to Jeff. "Spies? Just because they're Russian? Aw, that's old. Anyway, no one would send spies to U-Lab. There's no secret research going on. Dad has scientists from all kinds of places working on his experiment. Why should these guys be any different?"

Jeff danced up and down the driveway, the

basketball drumming a rapid beat on the cement. "Look, there are secrets and secrets. Sure, none of the *experiments* are classified stuff. But *my* dad says there's a lot of computer technology that's still supposed to be off-limits to the Russians." The ball arced once more into the hoop. *"Technology* is the big stuff these days. They could be after that."

Mark retrieved the ball and dribbled it down the drive, frowning. Jeff's dad ran the computer department at the lab; he should know. "Could be," he admitted. "But anyway, what does all the spy stuff have to do with my problem? *My* problem is that for eight weeks I'm going to have to spend every Wednesday afternoon baby-sitting Meg. Even if I didn't have to take her over to Natasha's, it still would be a drag."

Jeff snagged the ball from him, darted toward the hoop, and shot once more. "Lighten up! The chance to snoop around that house could make the whole thing exciting! How many kids get to spend hours and hours in the house of someone who might be a spy? And listen, another thing—Wednesdays I have soccer practice, so it isn't as though we could do anything, anyway."

Mark raced after the ball, caught it on the first bounce, shot it back to Jeff, and shrugged. "*You* have soccer practice," he said.

Jeff aimed once more, this time with both hands. Mark never could get used to how easy everything looked when Jeff did it. For an instant he forgot about the problem of Wednesday afternoons. The ball went in so gently it might have been in slow motion. Beautiful! He ran to get it.

"What I'm trying to tell you," continued Jeff, "is that you could try to do a little counterespionage work. You have a chance at a real inside position—why not see what you can find out?" When Mark tossed him the ball, he generously threw it back and moved aside so that his friend could shoot.

"Maybe you're right," said Mark. "But it's still a drag." He shot almost without aiming, but for once it went in.

Jeff headed home when dinnertime arrived, and Mark went inside the house. His father

3

was working in the living room, and Mark tried once more. "Do I really have to?"

Dad knew what he was talking about. He looked up from his notebook and said quietly, "If your mother wants to take a computer course, then I think it's our job to make sure she gets to do it."

"My job, you mean," said Mark.

"I'm in this, too," Dad reminded him. "I can leave the lab in time to put something together for supper, but there's no way I can be there when you and Meg get out of school."

When Mark shrugged and turned away, his father reached up to give his shoulder a gentle shove. "Be reasonable, Mark. A lot of kids have mothers who work. Just pretend this is a temporary day-care arrangement."

But the problem, thought Mark, was that he was the one doing the care. He would have to take his sister on the stupid bus out to the lab site, just so she could play with her stupid Russian friend there. And then he would have to walk her back, which was going to take a good half hour, and she would probably whine the whole way. And what was he supposed to do out there all afternoon, with two kindergarten babies and somebody's mother he didn't even know?

After dinner that night he lingered at the table as his mother cleared off the dishes. "It isn't fair," he grumbled.

"Look, I never said it was fair. I just said it was necessary," Mom responded. "I'm sorry, but that's the way it is. It's only one afternoon a week, and just for eight weeks." She carried the dishes off into the kitchen.

Mark could tell from the set of her chin that it was no use arguing. Still, when she came back for more dishes, he tried one last time. "Why couldn't she just ride the bus out without me?"

"You know she's too little to walk back by herself."

Mark had a sudden inspiration. "Dad could pick her up! He'll be coming home to make supper—he could just pick her up on his way."

Mom laughed and, for no reason he could tell, gave Mark a little hug. "Mark, your father is a physicist! It isn't just that some of the time he forgets how late it's getting. There are really days when he simply can't head home on time, because things are happening. If you get home before he does and you two are starved, you can always have a glass of milk. If worse comes to worst, I can get supper together when I get back." She gathered up the last few dishes from the table. "I can't expect Natasha's mother to keep Meg past five-thirty. She has her own family to take care of." Then, with what was clearly a final remark, she exited to the kitchen. "I think it was very nice of Mrs. Zhavoronkov to offer to entertain you both."

Ten minutes later Mark was behind the closed door of the den, bitterly quoting this last remark over the phone to Jeff. "Sure, *very* nice of Mrs. Whatever-her-name-is. And what am I supposed to do there for two hours? There aren't any kids our age out there, and Natasha's mother probably doesn't even speak English."

"Natasha speaks pretty good English," Jeff reminded him.

6

"Yeah, but she didn't when she first came, and everybody knows little kids like that pick up languages faster than adults. No, it's going to be a real drag—cooped up eight whole afternoons with a couple of silly girls and some dumpy Russian lady. Some entertainment!"

"Hey," said Jeff. "They're *Russians*. That's what I've been trying to tell you! This is a real chance. Look, doesn't it strike you as odd that only one of the Russian scientists came here with his family? The rest of them all had to leave theirs back home. Natasha's father must be some kind of Party big shot. I bet he isn't really over here to work on the experiment at the lab. He's just been slipped in with the real scientists, to get computer secrets. That sort of stuff goes on all the time."

Mark had never thought about why the whole family was here. Maybe there *was* something different about Natasha's father. "You really think so?" he asked.

"Sure," Jeff assured him. "You keep your eyes open."

"Why not?" said Mark, feeling more cheerful. He didn't want to admit he wasn't sure

7

what kind of clues a computer spy might leave around. But the idea of having something important to look for made him feel a little better. It always helped to talk to Jeff. Spending Wednesday afternoons on a counterespionage mission sounded a lot better than spending them baby-sitting. It was too bad they couldn't go together, he and Jeff. One of them could distract the mother while the other one looked for clues. But still, if something was going on, and he could discover it all by himself . . . Jeff was right. This was a special chance, and he should stop grumbling.

But his misgivings returned the first Wednesday, when he climbed onto the minibus to the lab behind Meg and Natasha.

He had gone out on the bus plenty of times before, but always riding all the way to the Roundhouse, where his father worked. Going there made him feel important. The famous gleaming cylinder stood tall against the prairie sky, its four bridges curving above the wide moat. He loved riding up on the elevator to his dad's floor and looking out the office window at the huge accelerator ring that traced a giant circular mound on the prairie below. Mark was proud that Dad was part of Uhlenbeck Accelerator Center. This was where the best physicists from all over the world came to run experiments together.

But Visitors' Village, where they were headed now, sat nearer the edge of the big site, far from the glamorous Roundhouse. There was nothing there but houses. And usually the visiting families just had really little kids, not older ones. Mark looked around the bus, checking out the age range of those aboard. None of them looked older than about second grade. And now it had started to rain again, a cold spring rain. They *were* going to be cooped up. This was clearly the start of a long afternoon.

Still, he told himself, it was an afternoon that might, just might, be the start of a trail to something important. He had never heard of anyone his age uncovering a spy. Jeff always saw the exciting possibilities; having a best friend like him was something special.

Even the way he *looked* was special. Jeff's hair was dark red, his skin a clear golden tan. Mark's hair was just ordinary brown, but he was the one who freckled. Jeff's smile was a flash of perfect white teeth; Mark knew *he* was going to have to wear braces next fall. And there wasn't much that Jeff couldn't do. He was really smart, he was already a star in almost every sport at school, and he could play just about anything by ear on the guitar. The only thing Mark was good at was school-work. It was real luck that they'd both moved here at the same time last summer. The other kids had been together since kindergarten. They all had their friends.

Maybe he and Jeff could have spent at least *this* Wednesday afternoon together, anyway, Mark thought. Probably soccer practice would have been canceled because of the rain. Well, too late to worry about that now.

As the bus made the turn into Visitors' Village, Mark peered through the rain-streaked window, watching the house numbers. Only their different numbers and colors distinguished the village homes. They were all the same shape, little Monopoly houses somebody at the lab had decided to paint ridiculous colors. There it was, number twenty-six, a gaudy red one. I've probably been kidding myself, thought Mark. Nothing exciting is ever going to happen in a dinky house like that!

The bus pulled to a stop half a block later. Meg looked back as she and Natasha stood up to get off. Mark nodded to show he knew this was the stop, glumly sheltered his books under his raincoat, and got off after them.

"Come on, it's this way!" called Meg, racing through the puddles with Natasha toward the red house. Mark slogged behind them, in no hurry to reach that door.

2

Natasha's mother must have been watching for the bus, for as they neared the house she flung open the door and stood with her arms spread wide, ready to give Meg and Natasha half a hug apiece.

She wasn't at all what Mark had expected. Somehow he had pictured her as dumpy and grim. In blue jeans and a big sweater with broad blue-and-white stripes, she instead looked trim and, well, American. He never would have guessed that she was Natasha's mother, either. Natasha was small and quiet, with sleek brown hair cut neatly short. The mother was tall, with a tawny mass of untidy hair framing her face. There was none of Natasha's reserve in her expansive welcome.

Mark waited apprehensively to see if she was going to try to hug him, too. He had seen his dad greeted by some of his European colleagues that way. Maybe it was the custom, and he'd have to put up with it. But as the girls ran past her into the house, she merely extended her hand and said, "You are Mark? Please, come in."

Mark shook her hand, feeling very formal. He knew he should say something in response. "It was nice of you to invite us over, Mrs. Zha—Zha. . . ." He could feel his face turning crimson. But how was he supposed to remember a name like that?

Natasha's mother seemed to understand. "ZHA-vor-on-kov," she pronounced clearly. "But I think our name is very difficult for Americans," she added, leading him into the house and starting to collect all the wet raincoats. "My name is Olga. Please, you call me Olga."

Mark noticed with surprise that Meg and

Natasha, who had already wiped their shoes carefully on the mat, were both now taking them off and setting them on the rug near the front door. Two pairs of small cloth slippers were waiting for them there, and beside those a pair of women's shoes was neatly placed. Glancing at Olga's feet, he saw she wasn't wearing shoes, just those soft cloth slippers. Oh, for Pete's sake, he thought. I guess I have to take off my shoes, at least. I thought they only did this in Japan.

Feeling a little silly, he untied his shoes and put them in a row with the others. Meg and Natasha had disappeared by the time he finished—to Natasha's room, Mark supposed. Natasha's mother—Olga—finished hanging up the coats and looked down at his stocking feet. "You will be very tall man," she said. "Your feet are already big like mine. I think maybe these will fit." She reached up onto a shelf above the coats and found another pair of slippers. Mark slipped his feet into them; they did fit.

Then for a moment, the two of them just stood there. Olga was still smiling, but it looked as though she, too, didn't know quite what they were supposed to do next. Mark suddenly remembered his books, there on the floor next to his shoes. "Uh—Olga—I brought some homework with me. Maybe if there is a table where I could work, I could just do it while you—"

Olga's face brightened. "Very good idea!" she said. "I also have homework. We will study together." She led him to the dining area and waved at a chair. "Please, sit down." As Mark did so and started to spread out his books and papers, she stepped into the kitchen and returned with a small dish full of paper-wrapped candies. "Russian chocolates," she announced, placing them before him, and then went off again to get her own books.

Mark picked up one of the candies and looked curiously at the paper wrapper. This certainly was a Russian chocolate; the printing was all in those funny Russian letters, and Mark couldn't even guess at any of the words. Cheap candy, thought Mark. Well, I suppose I have to be polite. He took off the paper and tried a bite. Not bad at all—the filling was creamy and crunchy at the same time. More like the chocolates that come in fancy boxes! He opened his math book and started in on the first problem.

Olga came back carrying a workbook and a lot of loose papers, with a pencil behind her ear. As she joined him at the table, she put her things down with a sigh. Mark was curious. "What are you studying?" he asked.

"English," said Olga. "I have English class at Roundhouse with other wives. For me, English very difficult." She gave a rueful shrug, opened her book, and set to work. Faintly, down the hall, Mark could hear Meg and Natasha chatting in high, artificial voices; it sounded as though they were playing dolls. For a long while the only sounds at the table were the scratch of pencil on paper and the occasional rustle of a chocolate wrapper.

When Mark finished his math problems, Olga was still checking over what looked like the same pages she had started on. Perhaps feeling his glance, she looked up and smiled.

"English *very* difficult," she repeated. "Please, maybe you look and see if all is okay?"

She passed the workbook to Mark, and he looked over what she had done. The exercise had to do with deciding in which order to put a string of adjectives within a simple sentence. Mark read the first sentence:

The florist selected _____ roses.

Below, there was a string of adjectives to arrange in order:

red beautiful three

He read how Olga had filled in the blank: "The florist selected three red beautiful roses." Mark frowned, trying to figure out what was wrong. "Um—I don't think that's quite correct. I'm not really sure *why* it's not; it just doesn't sound right. We'd say 'three beautiful red roses.' "

He turned back to the previous page in the workbook and discovered there was a chart showing how to order adjectives. "Hey, there are *rules*! I never knew that. Let's see. . . . Yeah, 'beautiful' would be a distinctive characteristic or quality, and that should come before color, not after." He studied the rules some more, then reached for his pencil. "Look, Olga, you can just give a number to each kind of adjective the rules talk about. Then you can decide which type each word is, and write the number under it. Here, I'll show you what I mean." He wrote a number under each of the adjectives for that first sentence, explaining carefully why each adjective should have the number he gave it. "Then all you have to do is write in the adjectives for the sentence, starting with the one with the lowest number and working toward the highest, and they'll be in the right order. Try it!"

He had to explain the rules to Olga a little more as she redid the next few sentences, but it was clear she had the idea. He sat back, watching while she concentrated on checking her entries using his system and correcting the ones that were wrong. It was funny feeling like a teacher—and with a grown-up student! Finally she finished and handed the workbook to him again. He skimmed down the list of sentences. "Hey, pretty good! They're all right except this one. See? 'Persian' is a proper adjective, not a quality, so it needs to come last. So that sentence would be 'The room had four old Persian carpets.'"

"You just know!" marveled Olga. "You not stop to think, not look at rules!"

"Well, sure," said Mark modestly.

Olga shook her head, brushed the hair back from her forehead, and made a little face. "*Never* will I be able to speak English as you do! But you are very good teacher, Mark. Now I understand how to do exercise correctly. And please, when I make mistakes talking, tell me. For me most difficult thing is to know how to use articles. In Russian we have no 'the,' we have no 'a.' I often do not know right place to say such words."

Mark couldn't help smiling. "*The* right place to say such words!" he corrected her. Olga hung her head and covered her eyes in mock embarrassment. "Now time for tea," she then announced, putting their books and papers aside.

Mark considered asking for milk or cola instead, but Olga was already beginning to set out teacups. Meg is too little for tea, he thought. Still, he didn't want to appear rude, so in the end he said nothing.

When Olga called the girls in, Meg didn't seem to be at all surprised to see the teacups, and Mark realized that probably she had been drinking tea whenever she visited Natasha. There were two separate teapots: one with strong tea, one with hot water. Olga gave all three children plenty of hot water in their tea, and with sugar it didn't taste bad at all.

A collection of other things had joined the chocolates on the table: a cake made of many thin layers with a cream filling, some small cookies, and a large dish of jam. What do I put the jam on? wondered Mark. But then he saw the others, even Meg, putting a little in a saucer and just eating it with a spoon. Weird, Mark thought, but he followed their example. The jam was bright yellow-orange, made out of some kind of berry he had never tasted before. The two girls talked quietly at their end of the table as they ate. To Mark's surprise, Meg seemed to have more grown-up manners here than she did at home. He couldn't help smiling to himself. My sister, the kindergarten cosmopolitan, he thought. Even knows the rules for a Russian tea!

3

Olga had a lot of questions about life in the United States; Mark tried to answer them as they slowly finished their second cups of tea. She was amazed by the fact that Mark already had moved three times, as his father first had taught physics at different universities and then come to the lab. "In Soviet Union sometimes you move to another city to study at university, but then you have your job, you work there. Very unusual to move to different job. Igor is at same institute always," she said.

Mark told her everything interesting he

could remember about California and New Mexico. He explained he was too little when they left New York to remember that, but he found he could still answer a lot of her questions about what the city was like.

"Haven't you ever traveled anywhere before, even just for a vacation?" Mark finally asked.

"Oh, yes," Olga said enthusiastically. "For vacation we go to Black Sea. Very beautiful there. You also travel for vacation?"

Mark described the vacation trips his family had taken to the Grand Canyon and Yosemite. "Of course Dad has been on trips to a lot of other places, a lot of other countries, too," Mark added. "He's been to Japan and Brazil, and to different parts of Europe. You know, for physics. Most of the time he goes by himself, but once in a while he can bring us. We all got to go with him to CERN last summer—that's a lab in Switzerland, but I guess you know that. A lot of physicists go to CERN. Has your husband been there?"

Olga smiled a little and shook her head. "Maybe someday," she said. She hesitated and then shook her head gently again. "This Igor's first trip to West. We very lucky. I get permission to leave job to come also. Travel for us is not yet so easy as for you."

Mark hoped it hadn't sounded as though he had been bragging—but after all, he realized, he *had* been to a lot of places.

Olga was curious, too, about the computer course his mother was taking. "It is possible even for woman who already finished university, woman with family, to go back, study more?" she asked.

"Well, sure," said Mark. "Anytime. Men, too. My teacher, Mr. Bronson, started working on his master's degree this year. When we complain about the assignments he gives us, he just tells us about the papers *he* has to write. Don't people ever go back to school in Russia? Don't they have adult-education classes there?"

"Adult-education classes?" Olga repeated. "I know words, but . . . In my country, you are student, you finish education, then you work." She thought for a moment, her eyes fixed at some point in the distance. "I think

24

I, too, would perhaps like to be student again," she added.

"Be *a* student again. Anyway, you *are,*" said Mark. "Remember? You're learning English."

"Yes," said Olga, "and I like, even if difficult. But when I return, I think perhaps I cannot use English. I would like to learn other new things also."

As they talked, Mark grew puzzled by all the things about American life he had to explain to Olga, all the things that surprised her. She seemed perplexed when he told her that the house his family lived in had three bedrooms and a den. "Many Americans live in big houses?" she asked. "Not in apartments?"

"Well, some people live in apartments," he explained. "But not so many out here. In the city it's different, of course. But the towns around the lab have mostly just houses. There are some new condos, but the only real apartment house I can think of right off is that big one on the way to Pinehurst."

"I have not been to Pinehurst," said Olga softly.

Mark stared at her. Pinehurst was one of the closest of the small towns that ringed the lab site. She could almost *walk* there. Well, bicycle, anyway, if she had a bicycle. How could she never have been there? It was almost as though she had just arrived—yet he knew the family had been there since before school opened.

"Don't you have other American friends?" he finally asked. "Haven't you visited anywhere outside the lab?"

Olga answered carefully. "I know some people, but it is not easy to make friends. My English is not so good. Here in village are other families, and some wives I know from English class. Meg comes here to visit Natasha, and so I meet—met?—your mother. But I have not car. Our Russian men are four, and there is one car for all. My husband works very many hours at experiment. We go to supermarket for food, and some days we go to shopping center." She paused, and again her eyes grew wistful. "Other wives sometimes say to me, 'Come, we go to city,' but I must be here for Natasha, so I say no." She sat silent for a long moment. Mark did not try to correct her English.

But then she smiled at him. "It is good that you will come with Meg these weeks. I am happy to have new friend. You can teach me about America, and maybe you have questions about Russia."

"Well, you're already teaching me to eat in Russian," said Mark, helping himself to more jam, and they both laughed.

Meg had to remind him when it was time to start for home. The rain had stopped, and Meg kept up with him without whining. Mark looked down at her thoughtfully as they walked. She hadn't done anything bratty all afternoon. At home, when Natasha came to play, Meg sometimes seemed to boss her Russian friend around. This afternoon, although Natasha's voice still had been quiet, it was she who clearly had been the leader in what they did, and Meg actually had listened to her ideas. Not a brat all the time, thought Mark tolerantly. In fact, Mark realized, the whole afternoon hadn't been what he'd expected. Even if he couldn't uncover any clues, it might not be so bad, coming here every week.

Dad was already home when they got there, putting together a dinner of pizza and a tossed green salad. Mom got home a few minutes after they did, and they all sat down to dinner.

"Looks terrific!" Mom smiled at Dad and unfolded her napkin. Then she turned to Mark. "Everything go all right this afternoon?"

"No problem," he mumbled, and dived into his pizza just as though he'd had nothing to eat all day.

"That walk home really gave you and Meg an appetite!" Mom said happily, watching him eat.

Mark and his sister caught each other's eyes for an instant, each giving the other a look that said not to mention that cake or those chocolates. It was hard not to grin. Mark reached for his napkin and solemnly wiped his mouth. Meg looked innocently at the opposite wall.

Okay, thought Mark, so maybe he had actually enjoyed himself—but he still hadn't met the husband. Igor, she had said his name was. He felt pretty sure Olga wasn't mixed up with anything fishy. How could she be? She almost never got out of the village, and she didn't know anyone. Of course, he told himself, maybe all that could have been an act. But he didn't think so. Anyway, she wouldn't have any reason to visit the areas at the lab where there might be computer secrets. She'd stand out like a sore thumb. People would notice her and ask questions. But Igor—Igor could probably be all over the lab, and no one would think twice about it. Igor was the one to keep an eye on.

4

The next afternoon, as soon as he had dropped off his books at home, Mark biked over to Jeff's. Even if he hadn't uncovered any great spy clues yet, he was looking forward to telling Jeff about his afternoon out at the village.

He pulled his bike up onto the porch and rang the bell. The door immediately swung wide open. Jeff, wearing a voluminous cape with a stiff collar that stood up behind his neck, lifted his arms to create wings of scarlet silk. Then he turned in a circle, the full folds swirling around him. "How about that, huh?

Dad was Dracula last Halloween. He said I could have it now."

Mark blinked. "It's great," he said cautiously. "But it's nowhere near Halloween, so what . . . ?"

"Dungeons and Dragons, you dodo," Jeff said, grinning. "I figure I can get into playing Undolph, the fearless warrior, a lot better if I'm dressed for it! Hey, how did it go yesterday with the Russians?"

"Well, it actually was kind of interesting," said Mark. "I haven't come across any computer-secrets stuff yet, but at least it wasn't a drag. I even found out something weird when I was helping Olga with her homework. Did you know there are *rules* about the way you order adjectives?"

Jeff made a face. "Spare me the grammar lessons! Look, what's the matter with you? I send you off looking for excitement, and you come back wanting to tell about how Olga from the Volga does her homework. Who's Olga, anyway? I didn't think Natasha had a sister."

"Oh, she's Natasha's mother." Mark followed him into the living room, feeling a little irritated. Jeff didn't even know who Olga was; he had no reason to make fun of her name.

"The mother? What's *she* doing homework for? No, I never said that. Forget Olga's homework. Time for adventure!"

Even though the game was Mark's favorite, for once he didn't feel like playing. "I haven't thought out a new dungeon yet," he objected. "If you want me to be Dungeon Master again, I have to plan it out some, ahead of time."

"Of course I want you to be Dungeon Master again!" Jeff assured him. "Hey, you're the greatest. But look, couldn't you just sort of make it up as you go along? I thought we'd get started this afternoon. Then on Saturday I'll get Mom to lay in the soda and potato chips, and we can really go for it. Providing I don't get creamed by one of your monsters today, of course." He gestured toward the table by the sofa. "Everything's ready, all the stuff we need. Come on!"

Mark walked over to the table and sank into one of the chairs that flanked the sofa. Jeff really didn't understand some things. He reminded himself that Jeff didn't know the game very well yet. So far they only had played once together, and Mark had been careful that the enemies Jeff's character battled weren't too powerful. But they shouldn't be stuck in two-person games forever. This game was supposed to have a regular band of adventurers.

"Listen, I think that before we play any more we should see if we can get some more guys. It makes it better if you have more characters. You really don't need more practice games. You know the rules now, and your character has some experience points. And you have lots of treasure from last time; you can buy all the equipment you'd need for a really complicated adventure. Maybe we could get . . ." He suddenly realized that he couldn't think of who else they *could* get to play with them. He was used to spending all his time just with Jeff.

"Aw, we don't need anybody else," said Jeff. "You want a more complicated adventure? Well"—his voice became deep and commanding—"you have here not only Undolph, he of the strong arm and fearless heart!" He caught up the edge of the cape, swirled it across his body, and curtained the lower part of his face behind the crook of his elbow. "You have Greyfog!" he intoned. "Armed with but a simple dagger and his powerful spells, the mightiest of magic-users!" Then he whipped off the cape, combed his hair over his forehead with his fingers, and hunched his back a little. "You also have light-fingered Leroy, the notorious footpad," he continued in a sinister whisper. "Curiously useful, if unreliable in the clutch."

Mark couldn't help laughing. There was nobody like Jeff! Maybe he *could* manage to invent a dungeon and its dangers as they went along, at least well enough so that Jeff would be happy. But somewhat to his surprise, he still didn't really want to.

Mark picked up some of the many-sided dice that lay on the table and poured them from one hand to another. "Look, you know more guys than I do. Can't you think of someone who might like to play this with us? We could get up a game for Saturday. That would give me time to get ready."

Jeff shrugged impatiently. "I don't know that many more guys than you do. Come on, let's *play.*"

"How about someone in your soccer league?" asked Mark.

"They're just guys I kick a ball around with," said Jeff. "I don't really *know* any of them."

"Well, this could be a way to start getting to know them," said Mark. "You could *ask.*"

Jeff folded his cape and laid it neatly on the sofa. Mark stopped playing with the dice and put them in a row on the table in front of him. For a moment, neither boy spoke. The tension in the air took Mark by surprise—but he was even more surprised when Jeff was the one who started to back off.

"Look, if you're tired of being Dungeon Master, you can just say so," he said. "No big deal. I never said you had to do that all the time. How about if I try it, and you can be the adventurer?" He picked up the cape again and, before Mark had time to protest, threw it across his friend's shoulders.

"Hey, I'd just look silly in that," said Mark. "I'm not the fighter type, anyway." He draped the cape over the arm of his chair. "When I'm a regular player, I'm usually a cleric. But really, it's not that I mind being Dungeon Master. I *like* being Dungeon Master. It's interesting, planning what's going to be there. And I know you could play half a dozen characters—that's not the problem. But . . . the real fun of the game isn't finding treasure and killing monsters and all that stuff. It's getting to *be* your character, not just playing him. And getting to know the other characters—figuring out how you can help each other and how much you can trust each other. If you play it that way, it makes the whole adventure more real." He glanced at Jeff's blank face and finished rapidly. "It just doesn't work if you're trying to be more than one character at a time. Look, I can start planning a really special dungeon, and we can both keep an eye out for new players. Okay?"

Jeff pulled his gaze regretfully from the

scarlet cape. "Okay, okay. Hey, I know what we can do—my dad finally got a flight simulator program. Want to go upstairs and try it out?"

"Sure," said Mark. "But listen, don't you really want to know about yesterday?"

"Not if it's just baby-sitting and grammar lessons," said Jeff firmly. "Look, you've only got seven weeks left, right? You've got to concentrate on looking for stuff that might be evidence!"

"We don't *know* that Natasha's father is a spy," protested Mark.

"But how can you really be sure he's not? Look, everybody is trying to get ahead of everybody else these days—Americans, Japanese, everybody. And the Russians are *desperate* for computer technology. You know if Natasha's father gets hold of something, he's not going to leave it around the lab. He'll think it will be safe at home. But *you'll* be there to find it."

"If I do," said Mark.

"You will, you will," Jeff assured him. "Just keep your eyes open. But spare me the details about the grammar homework. Come on, this is really a great program. Fantastic. You really feel like you're flying the plane."

Mark followed him up the stairs. It probably would have been hard to tell Jeff about yesterday in a way that would make it sound as interesting as it really had been, anyway.

The afternoon he had spent with Olga already seemed distant, as though he had eaten those chocolates in another world. Whether there were secrets hidden in that world or not, he was looking forward to going back next Wednesday. Being there was sort of like being Agoyan, the cleric, again—he felt taller there, and wiser. Only it wasn't an imagined world, it was a real one. Just different from his regular world. Meg was different when she was there—and so was he.

5

The next week the sun was shining when Meg, Mark, and Natasha walked up to the door of the red house. Olga was out in front, looking doubtfully at the space between the walk from the driveway and the face of the house. The narrow, rectangular space was filled with gravel. "Hello!" she said. "I happy to see you. Look—I want to make garden, but how?"

"Want to make *a* garden," said Mark. "I don't know how. Maybe you could put plants in pots there."

"Maybe," agreed Olga. She looked again at

the space, narrowed her eyes a second, and then nodded happily. "Yes, maybe!" They all went into the house. This time there were four pairs of cloth slippers neatly set out ready for them, and Mark knew the routine.

The girls soon put their shoes back on again, though, and disappeared into the backyard. Olga led Mark over to the table. "Maybe you like to help me," she said. "Natasha is learning American alphabet very well, but she does not learn Russian alphabet. I want to make cards to help her learn. Maybe it interesting for you?"

Mark had brought some homework with him again, but he could always do it later. "Sure," he said. "What do I do?"

"Here is book—a book—with Russian alphabet."

"*The* Russian alphabet."

"*The* Russian alphabet. I want to make letter on each card, then I can show her card and she say name of letter. You draw big letters, I draw little letters?"

"Okay," said Mark. The two of them sat

down together at the table, where Olga had already set out a stack of blank cards and some felt-tipped pens in different colors.

The first letter was simple enough. It was just like the English A. But the next letter was a Б. "What do you call this letter?" asked Mark.

"Beh," answered Olga.

Mark looked at the next letter, which was a В. "Then what's that?"

"Veh," said Olga.

Weird, but interesting. As Mark drew the different letters, he asked about the sound each made. As he suspected, the funny-looking Б was like an English B, and what looked like a В really acted like a V.

Some letters were simple: The Russian М was like an English M, and so was the Т.

Other letters were just unfamiliar shapes for familiar letters. Д was really like a D, Ф was like an F, and the letter И—which looked like a backward N—really sounded like an I.

But there were some confusing surprises.

The Russian H was really an English N, the Russian P was an English R, and the Russian C was like an S.

One letter looked like two letters: ы. It made another kind of "I" sound. On the other hand, some Russian letters stood for sounds that would take more than one letter to write in English. Mark especially liked the shape of Ж, which stood for a sound like "zh." Olga told him that was the initial letter of her husband's last name. She wrote the whole name for him in Russian letters:

ЖАВОРОНКОВ

When they had finished making the cards, Mark got a piece of paper from his notebook and copied the Russian alphabet in a column down the page. Then he tried to write down the sound each letter made. Olga helped. There were a couple of symbols that didn't really seem to be letters. Olga tried to explain to him how they changed the sounds of the letters they came after, but it was too complicated. He decided just to leave them off his list. Some letters could really stand for more than one sound, Olga told him. Still, together they figured out a way to describe the most common way of pronouncing each letter.*

After they finished the list, Mark looked at it a long time. "But how do you write down the sound of 'th' in 'thing'?" he asked. "Or 'w' in 'way'?"

"These sounds we do not have in Russian," explained Olga. "If you want to write American word like 'the' in Russian letters, maybe you choose letters that sound most like. Maybe you can write 'the' *so.*" Reaching for a blank card, she wrote:

Зэ

Mark looked at the card, thinking. If you wanted to write American words in Russian letters—he looked carefully at his list of letters—you couldn't just substitute letters. You'd have to think about the real sounds in each word, then figure out the way to write

*There is a copy of Mark's list at the back of this book.

them. "Wait a minute," he said. He took another of the blank cards. "Don't look at what I'm doing until I tell you," he commanded Olga.

"Okay," said Olga. "I go make tea."

Mark worked quietly for a while, then carried the card into the kitchen. He gave it to Olga without saying anything. Olga looked at the card, at first with puzzlement.

КЭН Ю РИД ЗЫС?

Suddenly she burst out laughing. "Yes! I can read this!"

It worked! A great new secret code! Now, *this* would interest Jeff. Maybe it wasn't computer secrets, but it was exactly the kind of thing he liked. No one at school would be able to figure this one out—just the two of them. If somebody found a note they had been passing back and forth, it would still be private. He could hardly wait to teach Jeff the code.

And who could tell? Maybe today he'd be able to stumble across the evidence that Jeff was waiting for. After all, the afternoon wasn't over yet.

A bit later, after he and Olga had cleared away the papers and were starting to put things on the table for tea, Meg and Natasha came bursting in from outside. "Mama! Mama!" cried Natasha, and a rush of Russian words followed. Mark had never seen her so excited.

Meg, behind her, held something cupped in her hands. "Look!" she cried, opening them a little. There lay a baby bird. At first glance Mark was afraid it might be dead, but just then it lifted its head and opened a beak that seemed three sizes too big for such a tiny creature. The noise it made sounded almost like a meowing cat—and a pretty big cat at that. It was hard to believe that such a loud noise was coming from so small a bird.

"Oooh," said Olga softly, bending over Meg's hands. "Only baby. It hungry."

"It *is* hungry," Mark said automatically. He still felt uneasy. He remembered hearing Mom tell how, when she was a little girl, she had once found a baby bird and done her best to raise it. It had lived for only one day. "What can we feed it?" he asked.

"I find some things," said Olga confidently. "You make nest for bird."

Mark found a wide soup bowl in the cupboard and sent Meg and Natasha after some tissues to pad it with. He started to put it on the table, but Olga called over her shoulder, "Put nest on floor—on *the* floor. Bird maybe can walk out of nest, can fall."

On the side of the table away from the kitchen, the children found a safe corner where no one would be likely to step on the "nest." They tried to settle the baby bird in its new home. It was squawking more and more loudly.

"Okay, little one," said Olga. "Here is dinner." On a plate, she had put some raw hamburger and some bread softened with water. She showed the children how to make tiny pellets of each. Every time the bird opened its beak, one of them popped a bit of food in. Then Olga brought a glass of water and a teaspoon and showed Mark how to feed the bird sips of water. Before long the tissues lining the nest were messy and soggy—but the baby bird was quiet. Mark sent the girls to get fresh tissues, and soon the bird was comfortably asleep in a dry nest.

"Do you think it will live?" asked Mark.

"Of course," said Olga firmly. "Many times I find baby birds. I feed them, they live."

Mark looked down again at the bird. The fragile-looking lids were shut and the big beak was closed, but he could see the tiny chest rising and falling slightly.

"Do not worry," Olga said. "Baby bird will not die."

"*The* baby bird will not die," said Mark.

Saying it made him feel better.

6

Mark had been right; Jeff loved the code. This time he was willing to let Mark tell him about what had happened at Olga's. He laughed when Mark imitated the raspy squawk of the baby bird, and didn't interrupt as Mark described how they had fed it. When Mark finished, though, Jeff shook his head. "Just remember, you're not there to baby-sit birds, either. If there's some secret stuff stashed somewhere, it's going to be in that house. Look, no one else has the same chance—it's up to you!"

All that next week Mark reminded Meg to

ask Natasha how the bird was doing. A couple of days Meg forgot to ask, but when she did bring back an answer, it was always that the bird was all right. No details, though. Mark was glad when Wednesday came. He barely said hello to Olga when she answered the door. Tugging off his shoes as fast as he could, he raced to the corner where they had put the nest.

There was the nest—but it was empty! Mark's heart gave a lurch, and he looked up at Olga. Seeing his face, she quickly touched his cheek. "The baby bird is okay, Mark," she assured him. "Look!" Mark didn't even need to follow her pointing finger, for just then the bird came out from under a nearby chair, squawking more loudly than ever, clearly demanding food. "And please notice: I remember to say 'the,' " added Olga proudly. "You see, I am learning. I study hard every day. Now we must feed little Vaska. Always he is hungry."

"So he has a name now," said Mark. "Vaska? Does it mean something in Russian?"

Olga laughed. "Vaska is name we give to cats in Russia. Natasha says that bird makes noise like cat, so we name him Vaska."

"Makes sense," said Mark. "Okay, Vaska—feeding time."

Natasha fetched the plate Olga had ready for them, with its mounds of soggy bread and ground meat. The two girls sat together on the floor and began to feed Vaska.

"What kind of bird is he?" asked Mark. "Do you know?"

"I think he—wait, I look in dictionary." Olga pulled an old blue book down from the shelf, bent over it a moment, ran her finger down a list of Russian words, and then silently sounded out the English word she was seeking. She looked up. "Starling—I think he starling."

"He *is a* starling," corrected Mark.

As fast as one of the girls could form a little pellet, Vaska ran over to gobble it up. It was amazing how much such a little bird could eat, and how fast he could run from one hand to another. Still he continued complaining, crying plaintively for more.

Just then a tall figure sleepily lumbered in from the hall. "I think you must be Mark, Meg's big brother. Please excuse that I am not yet awake; the experiment is running now and I was working all night." Dr. Zhavoronkov's dark hair was wet from his shower, but his broad face was still creased with sleep and heavy with fatigue. He came around the table and bent down over the bird. "I think little Vaska is not satisfied with these first courses; he must now be wanting the main course." Taking a large spoon from the kitchen as he went, Natasha's father disappeared out the back door.

That's *him,* thought Mark. At last he was getting to meet the husband! This was the man who might be up to something. He didn't look much like a spy right now, but, Mark reminded himself, looks didn't necessarily mean anything.

Dr. Zhavoronkov returned a few moments later carrying a worm in the bowl of the spoon. "Okay, little Vaska," he said, lifting the bird in his large hand. Vaska sat expectantly in his palm and opened his beak. Picking up the worm, Natasha's father pushed it firmly down Vaska's throat with his finger. Vaska gave a sort of hiccup, blinked, and settled down to sleep. Dr. Zhavoronkov watched him a moment, the bird cupped gently in his hand. Then he lowered him carefully into the nest in the corner, went back to the kitchen to wash his hands, and returned to the table, where Olga had fresh tea and rolls ready for him.

Mark, crouched next to Vaska's nest, watched out of the corner of his eye as the tall man ate. Natasha's father was chewing his food slowly, his gaze seemingly fixed on the opposite wall. Although he didn't actually look anything like Mark's own father, Mark recognized the expression on his face instantly. When Dad got that glazed-eyed look, it didn't matter *what* you said to him. You could tell him the house was on fire, and he would nod and say, "Um-hum," and go on trying to solve whatever physics problem it was he was working in his head.

Well, Mark realized, he should work on

some problems himself; he had math homework again. He got up and went over to get his books from the stand next to the door. Since the dining table was occupied, he decided to work at the desk in the living area. There was enough clear space on the desktop.

As he was opening his notebook, Mark noticed a tall stack of thick computer printouts on his left. This was exactly the sort of thing he was supposed to be keeping a lookout for!

Mark glanced over his shoulder. Olga was around the corner in the kitchen, the girls were not in sight, and Dr. Zhavoronkov's gaze was as preoccupied as ever. Gently, as if he were just making an absentminded gesture while he thought about his homework, he riffled through the accordion-folded stack. Pages and pages of scientific symbols and numbers! Mark's stomach sank. This was probably just what computer secrets would look like. Of course, Dad sometimes had printouts around that looked a lot like these, just analyses of data from the experiment. But surely they wouldn't have a Russian working on the computer part of the experiment. Not if computer technology was such a sensitive area.

He felt dismay rather than triumph. Natasha's father seemed like a nice guy, and just as important, he seemed like a real physicist. Mark had never seen that special glazed-eyed look on anybody but his dad and a few of the physicists he worked with, ones his dad thought were really good. A physicist who was a spy wouldn't be that wrapped up in his work—he'd have his mind on other things. But perhaps he was just being fooled. Maybe instead of working on a physics problem, that big man with the kind-looking face was really trying to figure out how he was going to sneak this stack of secret programs past the inspectors at the airport.

If the husband was up to something like that, was Olga in on it? Mark couldn't believe it. And suppose something funny really was going on—how would she feel when he unmasked her husband?

Of course, Mark reminded himself, he wasn't really certain that anything *was* going on. But how could he be *sure* that whatever was in these printouts was something a Russian should have? That Natasha's father was the nice guy he seemed to be? He remembered Jeff's words: *That sort of stuff goes on all the time.* And Jeff was in a position to know; he'd hear things from his dad. This could be important, and it didn't matter how he felt about it—he'd have to tell Dad. He bent his head over his homework and tried to do each problem as slowly as possible. How could he talk to Olga or her husband now and still seem natural? It was a relief when it was finally time to head home.

After dinner that night, Mark told himself he couldn't put it off any longer. Slowly he headed for the den. He was in luck. Dad was alone, and he wasn't working with his notebook, just sitting with his feet up, reading some book. Mark walked around the room once, picked up a magazine, put it down. "I met Natasha's father today," he finally said.

"Um?" said Dad, not really looking up. He wasn't making this easy.

"He had a great big stack of computer printouts on his desk," said Mark.

His father nodded. "I bet he did! Poor guy was up all night on the computer, after a full day shift at the accelerator. But none of us could figure out why we were getting such crazy results when we tried to analyze the first run."

"He's doing computer stuff for the experiment?" said Mark.

"At this point, I'd say most of it," said Dad. "He phoned me this morning before he went to bed—he finally got the program to work. I thought we'd never get the bugs out! Igor's an absolute wizard." He sighed contentedly and went back to reading his book.

"Oh," said Mark.

He retreated to his room, grateful that he hadn't gone ahead and made a real fool of himself. It seemed that the lab computers weren't off-limits for Russians after all. In fact, it even looked as if Natasha's father was the one who knew all the special computer tricks. Mark wasn't sure how he was going to tell Jeff about this. So much for their great counterespionage mission. Hah!

In a way, it would have been great if those printouts really had been stolen secrets. Jeff would have been impressed. Maybe Mark even would have been in the newspapers. But it would have been awful for Olga. And there wouldn't have been any more Wednesday afternoons.

Who needed all that spy stuff, anyway? It was worth going out there to see that crazy bird, a bird that ran around like a dog or something, a bird that wasn't scared of anyone. Maybe someday he should go out there *not* on a Wednesday—so that Jeff could come, too. Well, Jeff likes to make the plans, he thought. If he says he wants to go out there, we'll go. It was funny, though. In a way, he hoped the idea didn't come up.

It turned out that Mark needn't have worried about how he was going to break the news to Jeff that there was nothing to support their suspicions. That took care of itself. The very next day after school, the two friends were at a table together in the library. In theory they were working on reports for history, but actually they were practicing their new code. Jeff wrote in his notebook:

ДУ Ю ЗИНК ЗЭ ФАЗЭР ЫЗ А СПАЙ?

Mark read the sentence and smiled. He remembered the big hand cradling the little bird, and the sleep-creased face with that familiar look in the eyes. In his own notebook he wrote:

НО, А РИЛ ФЫЗЫСЬЫСТ!

Then he paused a long time, trying to figure out how to write "we were" in Russian letters. He couldn't. So finally he just wrote:

СТУПЫД!

and gestured quickly with his thumb first at his friend, then at himself. Jeff shrugged casually, just as though this outcome were what he had expected all along. Mark lowered his gaze to the paper in front of him and stared at it without really seeing it. Jeff had always seemed so *sure*! But then, Jeff could be one character one moment, another the next. Maybe this spy business had been just another game to him.

He gave his head a little shake and reached for the book lying next to his notebook. Without further exchange of messages, he and Jeff started to work in earnest on their history reports.

7

When Mark arrived at the red house the next week, Vaska looked twice as big as he had the week before. The bird was now scarcely ever in his nest. He followed Natasha or Olga around like a puppy, usually demanding food in his rasping voice. He still liked to be fed by hand, although by now he knew how to peck at food in a dish.

"Doesn't he ever get tired of eating?" asked Mark, as he watched the girls take turns feeding him.

"When he sleeps." Olga smiled. Mark wondered how Olga kept the rug so clean, but was embarrassed to ask how she cleaned up after a bird that certainly wasn't housebroken.

Vaska was starting to use his wings more, and if Mark held a piece of food above his head, he would flutter them as he tried to hop up toward it. "Soon he will learn to fly," said Olga.

"Aren't you afraid he might fly out the window or the door?" asked Mark.

Olga looked surprised. "But he *must* fly to the sky," she said. "The sky is his home. He is bird."

"*A* bird," corrected Mark absently, trying to understand. When you gave an animal a name, it was a pet. Wasn't it? And if it was a pet, you had to keep it safe, take care of it. . . .

But he had no chance to discuss the matter. Olga was busily starting to set out things to cook with. "Today I will be teacher for you," she said. "You teach me about many American things. I like to teach you something Russian. Today we make piroshki!"

The yeast dough was already mixed and rising. Mark scribbled recipe notes as Olga

showed him how to make two different fill-
ings, one from ground meat and one using
spicy cabbage. Before long she was rolling out
small circles of dough. The girls put blobs of
filling on the circles, and Mark was kept busy
pinching each circle into a little snack-size pie
and brushing it with melted butter. By the
time the delicious aroma of the first ones in
the oven began to fill the kitchen, Mark was
no longer thinking about what would happen
when Vaska learned to fly. The question on
his mind was how piroshki might taste with
chili added to the meat filling. Maybe with
cheese tucked in, too. Taco-flavored piroshki.
Why not?

Later that week, whenever the question of
what would become of Vaska began to surface
in his mind, Mark did his best to shove it
under again. A good trick was to think about
how to write hard words in Russian letters.
Sometimes it was surprising what was hard
and what was easy. A word like *clandestine*
would turn out to be a cinch, but he could still
not decide on the best way to write *that*. He

and Jeff both were practicing the code. They wrote all their notes to each other in it now, and they hardly needed to look at the list of letters anymore.

Mark didn't show the notes they wrote to anyone else—but their code didn't stay a secret. That Monday in the school cafeteria, Brad and Tim, who always sat in the corner, stopped at the table where Mark was starting his lunch. "Hey," said Tim, frowning, "do you and Jeff really know Russian?"

Mark blinked with surprise. Had Jeff shown them their notes to each other? Those notes were supposed to be private! Mark glanced at the two boys looking down at him. Did they think *he* was some kind of spy? Brad and Tim seemed like nice guys, but they certainly never had bothered to talk to him before.

He kept his voice casual. "Nah—we just have a sort of code that uses Russian letters."

"See?" said Brad to Tim. "I told you it was a bluff. Jeff's a show-off."

But Tim seemed to be thinking. "Real Russian letters or just pretend ones?"

"Real ones. I know a Russian family from the lab, and they taught me."

"Hey, neat," said Tim. "Is it hard to learn?"

"Only a little bit, at first," said Mark, relaxing. "After a while it seems easy." He hesitated a moment. He had thought of this as a private code for Jeff and himself, but there was no reason it had to be just that. Anyway, Jeff couldn't complain—he had let them see it. "Want me to teach you how it works?"

"Sure!" said Brad and Tim together. "After school today?" added Tim.

"After school," agreed Mark. The other two went on over to their corner to eat.

When Jeff joined him a moment later, Mark told him about the encounter. "Did you tell them you knew Russian?" he asked.

Jeff glanced at him, then quickly looked away again. "Aw, no," he said. "They just happened to see what I was writing and thought I did. I decided it was more interesting to let them go on thinking that." He glanced back at Mark and flashed a smile. "Life should be interesting, right?"

Mark shook his head. In spite of himself, he was smiling, too. That was Jeff; that was just the way he was. And he did make life interesting, you couldn't deny that.

Mark was surprised when Jeff didn't object at all to sharing the code with the other two. In fact, he seemed to think it was a great idea. They met the other boys after school and went over to Tim's house.

Brad and Tim caught on to the idea quickly. Keeping a copy of the key in front of them, they soon were able to figure out the notes Mark and Jeff wrote and to make up messages of their own. The notes they all wrote for each other started getting wilder and wilder, and pretty soon they were breaking up as they decoded them.

At the end of the afternoon, Brad wrote:

ЛЭЦ ДЭ ЗЫC АГЫН. ТУМАРРО?

and passed the note around. The other three read it, and one by one they nodded enthusiastically.

Tuesday was even better. When Jeff asked

Mark if he would plan a new dungeon so they could all go adventuring, it turned out that the other two boys already knew the game. They decided to set an all-afternoon Saturday meeting of what Jeff proposed be called the СУПЭР-СИКРЭТ СОСАЙЕТИ. Mark promised to have a new adventure ready by then. Even as he agreed, he was already planning how it could begin with the discovery of a mysterious note tacked to the dead oak tree, a note in a strangely familiar code.

That night Mark lay in bed looking back on the last two afternoons. The code was actually even more fun now that it wasn't just between him and Jeff. The other two boys had been impressed when Jeff had explained that the whole idea for the system had been Mark's. Jeff had been fair about that. He wasn't a show-off. That was odd, Brad's having called him that.

Yes, it had been a good idea to teach them the code.

It had been only a few weeks since that day when he and Olga had made cards so that

Natasha could learn the letters. But for Natasha it was different. For her, those letters weren't just something for a code—she could speak the real language that those letters went with. And English, too. It was funny to think about someone only in kindergarten who already knew what it was like to live in two countries. Maybe that was part of why Meg often seemed to look up to her. He and Meg had been to Switzerland, sure, but that was only for a visit, and unless people talked in English they hadn't understood anything.

Thinking about Natasha reminded Mark of Vaska. He felt again that twinge of uneasiness. What would happen when Vaska learned to fly? Determinedly shoving the problem to the back of his mind once more, he concentrated instead on his conversation with Olga about Mom's computer course. He should have asked her what she would want to learn if she could take an adult-education course. Maybe after Mom finished her course, she could take care of Natasha while Olga took a class.

But would there be time? Olga and her

family would have to go back to Russia eventually, but he didn't know exactly when. Maybe he shouldn't get her hopes up about taking a course. Probably the best thing would be to find out first from Dad how many more months Olga would be here. . . . Mark drifted off to sleep.

8

The next day Olga was waiting for them in the front yard with Vaska on her outstretched hand. "Watch!" she commanded the children. "Now fly, little Vaska!" She gave a flick of her hand and Vaska flew off, gliding all the way to the foot of a lilac bush several yards away. Then he ran back to the front door, clearly asking to be let back in.

Mark laughed. "He doesn't *want* to fly," he said. "He just wants to follow us around and be fed."

Olga looked surprisingly serious. "We have—how do you say it in English? Wait, I look in dictionary." She went into the house. Vaska slipped in with her, and Mark and the girls followed. After consulting the dictionary, Olga looked up and said firmly, "Spoiled. We have spoiled him. He forgets he is a bird."

Mark squatted beside Vaska and put out his hand. The bird immediately ran up his arm to sit on his shoulder. As he considered the implications of what Olga was saying, Mark could feel the little claws grasping through his shirt. Finally he protested. "But aren't you going to keep him? If you go on taking him outside, someday he just might fly away and not come back." Mark put his hand up to his shoulder, and Vaska gave his finger a little nibble. "Meg and I could take him when you have to go back to Russia. You know we'd take good care of him."

By now Meg, too, was realizing what was going on. "Aren't you going to keep him?" she asked, looking ready to cry. "Don't you like him?"

Natasha didn't say anything. She was looking at Meg rather than at her mother, her dark eyes sad.

Olga drew the girls over to the couch and sat between them, her arms around their shoulders. "Yes, I like him. But to like does not always mean to keep. If we keep Vaska, he cannot enjoy flying in the sky, he cannot have a wife, he cannot live a bird's real life. To keep would be only nice for us, not nice for Vaska."

"But it's not fair," protested Meg. "He wants to stay inside. He likes it with us."

"Yes, he likes it," said Olga. "But he came to our house only a baby; he does not yet know a bird's real life. It is our work now to teach him that life. It must be so."

Although her voice was very gentle, there was something about her tone that was familiar. Mark suddenly remembered hearing his mother say, "I never said it was fair. I just said it was necessary." He reached his hand up to his shoulder and gently stroked Vaska's sleek, warm body. Olga was right. "If you had wings, Meg, you'd want to be really free to use them."

Olga looked up at him gratefully, then tightened her arms around the girls' shoulders. "I do not think Vaska will forget us soon. Maybe he will return to visit us. But we must now teach him to fly, as we teached—taught—him to eat. A bird's real life is in the sky."

By the end of that afternoon, the girls were making a game of teaching Vaska to fly, squealing in triumph each time he achieved a new record for length of flight. Mark watched them as he helped Olga set out pots of yellow marigolds, half burying the pots in the rectangle of gravel next to the front door. He was remembering when Vaska, now a good-size bird, was so tiny that he could fit into even Meg's hand.

He didn't talk much. Olga, usually so eager to make conversation, was quiet, too.

That Saturday he met Tim and Brad at Jeff's, bringing the graph paper on which he had plotted out the new dungeon. The action, he had decided, would take place in the ruins of an old castle. A number of chambers enclosed an open courtyard cluttered with rubble, and there were yet more rooms in the labyrinthine lower level.

Mark was a little relieved to see that Jeff wasn't wearing his cape. A great cape, but he had a feeling that Brad especially wouldn't have gone for it. Anyway, Undolph probably wouldn't wear a cape. Capes were more for magic-users, not fighters.

Everything was set for a long afternoon. Jeff's mom had insisted on providing fruit juice instead of soda, but there was a gigantic bowl of potato chips, a backup bag ready to be opened, and a big bowl of pretzel sticks as well. The other boys spread out their record sheets and the paper they would need for mapping and figuring. Then they introduced one another to their characters. Jeff was Undolph, of course. Tim was the demihuman Glimrock, a seemingly delicate but powerful elf. Brad announced that he was Urro, a sturdy dwarven veteran.

It was clearly necessary to make some adjustments before they could begin real play. Jeff's character, Undolph, had an amount of treasure close to that of the other two—Mark realized he had probably been too indulgent when he was guiding Jeff through his solo adventure—but Glimrock and Urro far outranked him in experience points, and they both had collected a lot of items of magic. With difficulty, Jeff was finally persuaded that his character would need to accept some of those items as gifts from the other two. He refused to worry about the other imbalances, and finally they just decided to begin.

Glimrock and Urro helped Undolph choose what additional equipment he might need for the adventure and bargain for good prices in the village nearest the castle. Brad and Tim were really good at the game—they always talked as their characters, and after a few reminders, Jeff, too, remembered that it should be Undolph speaking, not he. Little by little, the adventure started to feel real. When they had to stop their drama—to shake the dice that determined the outcome of the action they had decided to take, or to add to the map they were little by little able to draw of the dungeon they were exploring—it was as though the frame of the action stayed frozen, waiting for them to return to the world they were creating.

Led by the fantasy that Mark had planned so carefully, the three characters cautiously approached the ruined castle. Its last lawful owner, the gentle Queen Lealorn, was still imprisoned—although cast in some unknown, enchanted form—within those dark walls. A mysterious message had been found, telling how she had been waiting through the centuries for a rescuer—a rescuer bold and determined enough to defy the curse left upon the castle by her enemy, the chaotic Maloverne, and to do battle with the many monsters placed there to defend the ruins.

The afternoon passed too quickly, as the adventurers progressed from one chamber to another, seeking clues to the location of the lost queen and to the form in which she was trapped. The most perilous battle took place in the open courtyard, where the party was attacked by the steel talons of Maloverne's giant falcon. Not expecting danger to approach from the sky, they were taken by surprise. Urro, gravely wounded early in the encounter, had to retire from the struggle. Undolph continued courageously, even recklessly, to do battle. The combined urging of the other two finally persuaded him to seek refuge with them inside the walls, where Glimrock could tend his wounds.

Just when they were trying to decide on their next move, as the great talons clawed to enlarge the opening through which they had slipped, the ring of a telephone shattered the spell.

"Tim!" called Jeff's mother. "Your family is waiting to start dinner!"

Mark looked at his watch. Six-thirty! Well, they would just have to continue another time. Quickly he totaled the treasure the party had gained, and, while the other three discussed its division, calculated the experience points each had earned. Then he, Tim, and Brad gathered up their papers and headed off to their homes.

I should have kept track of the time better, thought Mark. That wasn't a good place to have things just break off. Everything so uncertain, so unresolved.

He didn't know why he didn't feel more cheerful. The game had gone better than he would have dreamed; it was as if they had all played together a long time. And if you had to break, well, you had to break. Anyway, it had been a good session.

But walking home, he felt restless. It's the game, he thought. All those monsters, something dangerous at every turn. It makes you feel as though something bad is going to happen. Just the game.

9

When Mark reached the red house the next Wednesday, he found that Vaska already had become a skillful flier. He now spent most of the day out-of-doors, but he never went far from the house. He liked to perch in the big lilac bush near the front door or in the pine tree out in back. When the children or Olga came near, he often would fly down and sit right on their heads, squawking cheerfully. Sometimes he still demanded to be let into the house. They let him in, but Olga insisted that no one feed him there. "He knows now how to find his own food," she reminded them.

The day was warm, and she and Mark decided to do their homework on the grass under the pine tree. Olga seemed somehow distracted, quieter than usual, but Mark decided that maybe she just had an extra-hard lesson. He felt guilty. He had forgotten about asking Dad how long the family was going to stay. Maybe there still would be time to fix it up for her to be some other kind of student, taking something she could choose herself. He would have to remember to check with his parents and start seeing if it could be arranged.

Later they all had tea at a picnic table in the backyard. Vaska sat in the branches nearby, making occasional swoops down toward the food and scolding them indignantly when they shooed him away from their plates.

As they were finishing their tea, a man Mark hadn't seen before came around the side of the house—a short man with blond hair and thick glasses. On seeing them, he hesitated, then asked Olga a question in Russian. Mark thought he recognized the word *Zhavoronkov;* it sounded as if the man was asking if she was Mrs. Zhavoronkov. Olga stood up, and the beginning of her answer to him was *"Da,"* which Mark knew meant yes. The two shook hands and talked a minute or so longer, but Mark could no longer guess at what they were saying. Then the man handed Olga a small package tied up with a cord. Olga immediately thrust it into her apron pocket. The two shook hands again. The man nodded quickly at the children. "Good afternoon," he said in English. Then he hurried around the corner of the house and disappeared.

"Who was that?" asked Meg.

"He friend," said Olga. "He ringed—rang—doorbell, and when we did not come he followed voices here." She didn't say anything about the package, and Mark had the impression she was nervous about the visit.

What's going on? Mark asked himself. That wasn't any friend—he even hadn't been sure who Olga was. Maybe he was . . . But then Mark made a face at his suspicions. It was probably just a friend of Igor's, he thought, leaving something off for him. Why should I expect her to explain all about some guy who happens to drop by unexpectedly?

But why did Olga seem so nervous? Maybe Igor wasn't the spy—this man was. Maybe he was spying on Olga and Igor.

Mark smiled a little at that idea. Hey, he reminded himself, it's Jeff who specializes in making life interesting—forget about seeing spies everywhere!

"Maybe Vaska won't ever fly away for good," Meg said hopefully to Mark on their way home that afternoon. "He likes us."

Mark wasn't sure what he should say. He wished he could believe that Meg was right. "Well," he finally responded, "even if he does go away, maybe he'll come back. Remember, Olga said he might." But he reached down for her hand, and Meg didn't let go of his until they were nearly home.

That evening when Dad put dinner out on the table, he looked tired. As he sat down and unfolded his napkin, he gave the children a half smile that was more like a grimace. "Well, Meg, I'm afraid you're going to have to say goodbye to your friend Natasha sooner than we expected."

Mark looked up sharply.

"Why?" asked Mom, serving their plates from a big casserole. "The Russian group going back early?"

"Yes, two whole months sooner than we had expected. I was afraid of this when our idiot director decided to postpone the next run. They got a phone call from their institute last night. They're all as upset as we are."

"But how can the experiment finish without them?" Mom protested.

"Oh, the institute will send a new group over as soon as we get word that we can start up again, but it's a real setback." Dad frowned; he looked worried. "Even if the new group is as good as this one, it takes a while to learn the ropes. These guys were in on it from the beginning." He picked up a dish of green beans, put some on his plate, and passed the dish on to Mark.

Meg looked as startled as Mark was feeling. "Natasha is going back to Russia?" she asked.

"Why can't she stay longer? I don't want her to go!"

"Her family was just here for a visit, remember?" Mom reminded her. "We just didn't know they'd be going back quite so soon."

Mark slowly helped himself to the green beans. Olga must have already known this afternoon, he thought. Was it really a phone message that called them back? Maybe that man had something to do with it. . . . "How soon will they be leaving?" he finally asked.

"In about three weeks," said Dad.

Mark could see that his mother was quickly figuring something in her head. Then she nodded. "Well, anyway, that gives me time to finish my course. But we should do something special for the Zhavoronkovs; they've been so nice about watching Meg." She gave Mark a warm glance. "And of course it wouldn't have worked without *you.* I think I owe everybody a thank-you celebration. How about inviting them all over for a big farewell dinner?"

Mark paused. If the family came to dinner, the two fathers would just sit around talking physics, and the mothers would talk about the things mothers talk about. It wouldn't be the way it was on Wednesdays. He remembered Olga's wistful look when she talked about how seldom she got to travel off the lab site. "I bet it would be more fun for them to do something with us in the city."

"Good idea," Dad agreed. "I'll see if I can arrange the shifts so that Igor and I are both free a week from Sunday. We'll make a day of it."

"You know the whole family, Mark," said Mom. "Why don't you look at the papers this weekend to see what's going on in the city? See if you can spot something you think they'd especially like. And think about where we should go for dinner afterward. Maybe you'd like to invite Jeff, too?"

"No," said Mark before he had time to think. He glanced up and saw a look of surprise on his mother's face. He himself was a little startled by his own answer. "Well, he doesn't know them," he added. "He'd probably just be bored."

"What's this?" said Dad. "Tonto going off without the Lone Ranger?"

Meg was puzzled. "Who are the Lone Ranger and Tonto?"

"When Daddy was a boy," Mom explained, "there was a TV series about a sort of cowboy hero called the Lone Ranger. Tonto was his Indian helper."

"Daddy's being silly," said Meg. "Mark and Jeff don't play cowboys and Indians."

Mark could feel himself blushing and wished he knew how to stop doing it. He knew perfectly well what his father had meant. It didn't have to be a big deal if sometimes he wanted to do things without Jeff.

Mom seemed to feel the same way. "Daddy *is* just being silly. And you're right, Mark, I think it would be nicer just to have the two families."

That Sunday Mark studied the Entertainment section of the newspaper with care. It had a Dining Out column, as well as lists of movies, plays, and concerts. There were more choices than he had expected. It took him a long time to make up his mind, but finally he had it all worked out. He made a list of the things he thought they should do, then showed it to his mother. "That's perfect!" she exclaimed. "They'll love it."

"Good," said Mark.

But somehow he didn't feel good at all.

10

The next Wednesday when he arrived at the red house, Olga gave a hug to him as well as to the girls. He didn't feel embarrassed, but he didn't feel like hugging back, either. He knew why she did it. "Dad says you'll be going back to Russia soon," he said.

"Yes," said Olga. "We can talk about it in a minute. But please, all come now to the backyard. There is something to see."

She led them through the house and out to the picnic table in back. "Look!" she said, pointing up into the tree branches. A familiar squawk greeted them from above, but Vaska did not swoop down to their heads. Mark looked up. There on the branch next to Vaska was another bird, equally dark but a little smaller. "Vaska is not alone now," said Olga.

She doesn't have to be so happy, thought Mark. Now he *will* fly off for sure.

The girls stayed outside, watching Vaska and his new friend. Mark followed Olga back into the house and silently spread his homework on the table. He certainly wasn't going to stay outside.

"Igor says we will all go to the city together on Sunday," said Olga. "He says you plan a special day for us."

Mark told himself to stop being a rotten sport. He had known Vaska wouldn't stay. He made himself smile back at her. "Yeah," he said. "First we go up to the top of Hirsch Tower, because you said you'd never been up a real skyscraper. And then we go to the science museum, where they have all kinds of exhibits you can play with—even Natasha will like it. And then we have a picnic by the lake. And after that we go to the Supramax theater to see a film on the Grand Canyon, because you told me you wished you could see the Grand Canyon."

"What is Supramax theater?" asked Olga.

"It's like a movie theater," explained Mark, "except that the screen is really huge, and it curves—it curves around the sides, and it even curves above you. And the way the movie is projected makes you feel as though you are really *in* the picture." He reached for a blank sheet of paper and drew her a sketch so she would have an idea of how huge the screen was, and how far up it curved. "I went there once to see a movie about flying, and it was just like being on the runway with an airplane taking off, zooming right over me, or like really being a bird that was taking off from a cliff—so real it was kind of scary. Anyway, after that we go to a Mexican restaurant for dinner. Because you have never been to Mexico."

Olga looked away, and Mark was astonished to see that her eyes were moist. Her smile trembled a little. "It will be wonderful day for us," she said. "For me it has been like dream to visit America, and now I will also visit Grand Canyon and Mexico. You are very good to plan such a day."

Mark shrugged. There was something almost like anger sitting heavily in the pit of his stomach. "I didn't think it was such a dream for you here. You're stuck all the time out here on-site, aren't you? You don't get to go anywhere, and you don't have anything to do. Probably you miss your friends and your job. I guess you'll be glad to be getting back."

Olga nodded. "Yes, I miss friends, and sometimes I miss job. But when I am there I will miss America. I will remember little Vaska and also remember the afternoons you help me to learn English. Now it is not only Russia where I have friends. Igor, too, will miss his friends. For him, to work together on experiment with American colleagues has been good, very good."

Mark didn't say anything. If it was so good, why didn't they try to stay longer? He bent his head over his books. Olga stood there a moment longer and then went quietly into the kitchen to prepare tea.

The next afternoon, on the way home from

school, Mark told Jeff that the Zhavoronkov family would be leaving soon.

"It must be hard for Russian families to go back after living here," said Jeff.

"You kidding?" asked Mark. "Life here is just a lot of work for the husbands—and pretty dull for the rest of the family."

"Don't be dumb," said Jeff. "Don't you know anything about life in Russia? They probably have to live in some little tiny apartment back there and stand in line just to get crummy food. There's not much for sale in any of the stores, not stuff you'd really want."

"You sure it's that bad?" asked Mark.

Jeff nodded. "Dad has been there, and he says that almost nobody has his own computer, and that even in labs they're pretty scarce. He says that sometimes even really good physicists have to spend weeks and months doing big calculations by hand. It must be a *dream* for them to visit this country. I bet they wish they could stay."

Mark didn't answer. He remembered hearing Olga say, "For me it has been like dream to visit America." Maybe Jeff had been wrong the first time, about the spy business. Well, face it, he *had* been wrong. This time, though, he was probably right. Of course they must want to stay! He should have guessed that himself.

And why shouldn't they be able to? Mark knew from hearing his father talk that Igor was a good physicist. It shouldn't be hard for a good physicist to find a permanent job in the United States. Once they had a car of their own, Olga could go places and make friends. Natasha already spoke good English, and Olga didn't make so many mistakes now. It would be easy for them to get along—all they would need would be a little help at first. How could he have been so stupid?

But he didn't say anything more to Jeff. Jeff was his friend, but he didn't have to know everything. The Zhavoronkov family was supposed to go back to Russia; their government hadn't given permission for them to stay here. What Mark was starting to think about was helping the family to defect—and he knew that was a serious business. The fewer people that knew about it the better. He wouldn't even tell his own family until he had talked it over with the Zhavoronkovs.

It didn't take him long to work out all the details. The only real problem, after all, would be how to manage while Igor looked for a job. But Mark could sleep on the couch in the den and give his room to Olga and Igor. There was space in Meg's room for another bed; Natasha could stay there. It wouldn't cost much for the extra food they would eat, and it would only be for a little while. Dad would know how to help Igor get a job somewhere—maybe even at the lab.

And they wouldn't have to go back; Olga wouldn't have to go.

11

The secret plan was never far from Mark's mind; he could hardly wait to explain it to Olga. When Sunday came, knowing the secret he had ready for her made their day together seem even more special, like a promise of things to come.

And the day was indeed wonderful. Everything went exactly as he had hoped. He watched Olga's eyes widen as she looked from the observation deck at Hirsch Tower down to the street, nearly one hundred floors below. You'll get to see plenty of other skyscrapers now, he thought triumphantly. He listened to

Natasha and Meg squeal at the images on the Supramax screen. Gripping the arms of their auditorium seats, they were running the rapids of the Colorado River, down through the canyon. Maybe, thought Mark, we can all *really* visit the Grand Canyon together someday.

At the end of the day, in the brightly decorated dining room of Hacienda Alegre, Olga listened with shining eyes while a strolling guitarist sang Mexican songs at their table. As the guitarist moved on, Igor lifted his glass. "Please," he said, "I would like to propose a toast! To the friendship between our families, and to many other such times together in the future!" Mark knew Igor probably meant more visits some year soon, but as he sipped his orange drink, his own private toast was slightly different. To many such times together—a whole lot sooner than Igor thinks.

Mark's mother made the next toast. "To Olga and Mark!" she said. "Next Wednesday I finish my programming course, and thanks to you two I can start making plans for a brand-new career next fall!" And next fall, thought Mark as he took another sip, Olga can start taking courses of her own.

Then Olga tapped her glass with her spoon to show that she, too, wanted to make a toast. "To Mark, who planned this day!" she said. "All my life I dream to travel, but I never thought such dream come true. Now I have lived in America, I have learned English. But today is best day of all. All in same day I have seen many wonderful things—lake that is big like ocean, building that is tall like mountain. I have felt myself being in Grand Canyon, I have eaten dinner in Mexico. This day I will remember always. Always."

Mark smiled back at her, drained the last drops in his glass, and absentmindedly finished off the remaining fragments of the nachos. His mind was blissfully busy, sketching out yet more plans for the future.

It was hard to fall asleep that night, thinking of all the things they were going to be able to do. He wished there had been a chance during that day to tell his plan to Olga.

The next day, Monday, Mark saw not

Olga, but Igor. Dad had arranged to take all the Russian men on a shopping trip to the mall, and since Mark needed some new gym shoes, he was to meet them at the Roundhouse after school and go with them.

It felt funny to catch the minibus and not be going to the little red house. As the bus passed through Visitors' Village, Mark couldn't help looking out the window. Maybe Olga would be in the yard. She wasn't, but to his surprise Igor—who by now surely should have been waiting at the Roundhouse—was standing on the front steps. He was talking to a shorter man who was handing him an envelope.

As the minibus passed, both men turned to look at it. The second man was blond, and he wore glasses. It was the same man who had come into the backyard that other day and given a package to Olga. Mark decided that he probably had been right—the man was a friend of Igor's. But why was Igor at home instead of at the Roundhouse?

When Mark got to his father's office, the other three Russian physicists were there waiting. "Hi, Mark!" said Dad. "I'd like you to meet Sergei."

A thin, serious-looking young physicist shook his hand and murmured something Mark didn't catch.

"And this is Misha," Dad continued.

Misha was older, with a round face. "I am glad to make your acquaintance!" he exclaimed, pumping Mark's hand. "At home I have a boy just so big as you. Please, you will help me choose things he will like."

"And this is Nicolai," Dad concluded. Nicolai had curly hair and a wide grin, and he, too, shook Mark's hand.

"We may have to wait for Igor a bit," Dad went on. "He was finishing up some work, but he promised us he'd be here by quarter of four."

Igor hurried in a few minutes later, ten minutes earlier than promised. "You made it!" Mark's father teased. "I thought we'd probably have to go over and pull you away from that computer—you never know when to quit."

Igor looked embarrassed. He darted a

glance at Mark. He knows I saw him! Mark realized. But why is he letting everyone think he was at work all the time? Why is it such a secret that he went back to his house? Just who *was* that man? And what was in that envelope?

The six of them piled into the van and drove out to the mall. Mark got his gym shoes, then followed his father and the others around as the men chose things they wanted to take back to Russia with them. Mark tried on a series of down jackets so that Misha could choose just the right one for his son.

The Russians bought some video recorders and cameras and things for themselves, but they spent most of the time buying jeans and shirts and toys for their kids, and dresses and other presents for their wives. Mark realized he had forgotten that the other men had families back there. They must have missed them. It was like going shopping at Christmas.

At suppertime they had hamburgers together in the lower level of the mall. Mark noticed that just as he had learned to eat in Russian, all the Russian physicists had learned to eat in American. They dipped their French fries in catsup as though they had been doing it all their lives.

After their supper break, they made two more stops—one at a bookstore, another at a hardware store—and then agreed it was time to get back. Mark's father dropped the Russians off at the Roundhouse, where the car they shared was parked. Then the two of them headed back home.

Mark hadn't had much time to think that afternoon—but now he had to start figuring things out. What was all the mystery about that blond man? If he wasn't some sort of spy, what was going on? Mark was determined not to invent some kind of crazy story. Igor and Olga weren't just Russians; they were his friends. But something was going on, and he was equally determined to find out what.

"Dad?" he began. "How come Igor was doing so much stuff on the computer for the experiment?"

His father looked puzzled. "Because he was so good at it; I told you."

"But why aren't the computers off-limits to Russians?"

"There's nothing secret about the lab mainframes—anybody can use them."

"But Jeff said . . . Isn't there some computer technology that is off-limits to Russians? Some sort of computer secrets they might want to steal?"

His father snorted. "Oh, he must be thinking of supercomputers. Sure, you can *access* a Cray from here, but you'd need the password."

"So the only secret around here is the password?"

"That's right. But don't worry; nobody is stealing that."

And even if somebody could, thought Mark, it wouldn't look like a stack of printouts, or a package, or a big envelope. . . .

But something was going on. Something secret.

"How do you know when you can trust someone?" he finally asked.

His father didn't answer right away.

"Mostly," he said at last, "we like to trust our friends. But you can't trust anyone about everything, even the people you love best. Your mother could trust me with her life, but if she sends me to the store to buy a list of five things, she knows I probably will come back with about three of them."

"And she can't trust you to come home in time for dinner," Mark added with a grin.

"You got it."

Mark's face grew serious again. "But that still doesn't answer my question. I'm not talking about little stuff."

"Well, when something about trusting a person bothers you, it's usually because that someone is a friend."

Mark didn't say anything.

"And if that's the case, I'd say a first step might be to talk to the friend about what's bothering you."

Mark was grateful that his father didn't ask any questions. He thought over the advice. Maybe, he decided, it's that simple. Maybe I should just ask Olga. But first I've got to tell her about my plan.

12

He had his chance at last on their final Wednesday together, while the girls were outside hunting for Vaska. Vaska and his friend had been around the day before, but they hadn't been sighted since.

The house was already cluttered with cartons and suitcases. Mark wished it looked the way it always had. He suddenly felt less certain of how things were going to turn out. He drew a deep breath. "Listen, Olga," he started, "let's sit down. I need to talk to you. I've got a plan. . . ."

Olga heard him out without interrupting,

her face serious and intent. When he had finished, she paused a moment before responding.

"My friend Mark," she finally said, "I am very happy that you want so much for us to stay. I can see you have thought very hard to make such a plan. It is indeed true that many things in my country are more difficult than in America, many things. Our apartment there is more small, this is true. It has not so many rooms as this house. And indeed your shops are very different." She smiled faintly and shook her head. "When I tell friends in my own country of all the things in American stores, I think perhaps they will not believe me."

The words were okay, but Mark realized from her tone that she was beginning to say no. "You haven't even *started* to see America yet!" he interrupted. "Listen, I know that you haven't been able to travel around a lot while you've been here. But remember how it was last Sunday! Look, you could *really* go to the Grand Canyon! You could go to all the places I've told you about, you could go anywhere you wanted. We could all go down to Mexico, the real Mexico, not just a restaurant. You could go back to school, like Mom. You could do anything. You don't understand!"

"I understand," said Olga quietly. "But it is necessary that you understand, too; that you remember where is my real life, where is Igor's life, where is Natasha's life." She touched Mark's hand gently. "As you love America, we love Russia. Part of Russian life is still difficult, yes. But not all parts are difficult. Many parts are very good. Many things are changing—we work, we hope. Life in America, too, has some good parts, also some difficult parts. Please, understand."

Mark suddenly felt as if nothing around him were real anymore, as if she had already left. Everything he was saying was of no use. He couldn't believe it. "You said that you would always remember Sunday," he protested. "I wanted to make your whole life be like that!"

Olga paused, then said softly, "I will indeed remember that day you made for us always, all my life."

But she was still just saying no. Mark stood up and turned away, unsure now of what to say, what to do. He wished he could just disappear. All his plans!

Olga rose, too. She put one hand gently on his shoulder. "Please understand that we also are sad to say good-bye. But it is important that we return to own life, real life."

Mark stood silent for a moment, then turned toward her again. "Like Vaska," he said bitterly. In spite of what he had told Meg, he didn't think Vaska would ever come back.

"Like Vaska," responded Olga, "but also not like Vaska. Vaska is only bird—only *a* bird. Maybe next year he will return to this place and remember us, maybe not. When he is far away, he will not think of us. When a bird flies away, you have no bird. When a friend goes away, you still have a friend."

Mark tried to return the smile she gave him, but he couldn't.

"Or maybe you forget us?" teased Olga.

Finally Mark managed something like a

grin. "The minute you are on the plane," he threatened.

Olga's smile widened. She gave him a little pretend swat. Things started to feel more normal. Without more words, the two of them automatically began to set out the things for the now-familiar ritual of afternoon tea.

But there was still that other thing—the blond man. This wouldn't be easy, either, but Mark had to talk about it. He tried to sound as casual as possible. "Listen, there's something I've got to ask you. You know that man with glasses? The one who gave you a package, the one who was here with Igor on Monday? Who *is* he?"

Olga paused for a very long moment, the teacup in her hand hovering above the saucer on which she was about to place it. Then she put the cup carefully on the saucer and turned to Mark.

"Sometimes we have secrets even from friends," she said. "But not all secrets are bad secrets. Yes, Igor told me you saw him. He said you would maybe ask why he did not say to others he was here. Igor said if you asked, maybe I should tell you. I think yes, I should tell."

"Tell me *what*?" said Mark. "What's the big mystery?"

"Is not big mystery," said Olga. "Is very small mystery. Maybe silly mystery, not needed. Many things are changing, and maybe Igor and I are too careful from habit."

None of this made any sense to Mark, but he saw that there was nothing to do but let Olga tell it her own way.

"The man you saw is from Russia, but he now lives in United States, in city. He stayed here without permission—you say defected— five years ago. His brother is physicist, his brother is good friend of Igor. When this man stayed in United States, it made big problem for his brother, for all his family." She shook her head, remembering. "At first they are afraid brother would lose job at institute, family lose apartment. That not happen, but it is still for them a big problem." Olga turned up both palms in a quick gesture of frustration.

"How to explain? They think of him every day, but cannot send letters."

"Why can't they? Would someone stop the letters from being delivered?"

Olga paused, looking troubled. "Probably not, but it would be known they were writing to him. Government might think that they, too, wished to live abroad, in West. If physicist needs to travel to conference outside our country, maybe government not give permission." She sighed and gave a small shrug. "So better not to send letters in mail. When friends can bring letters, that is better. When we came here, we brought to this man letters from his brother, from his mother. Now we go home, we bring letters to them and present from man here to physicist brother. Here, I show."

She went over to the desk, opened a drawer, and lifted out the small package Mark remembered, together with an envelope. She untied the wrapping; inside was a man's watch. "It is difficult to find good watches in Russia," she said. "This will be very good present." Then she drew from the envelope pages of handwritten Russian and a stack of snapshots. Mark looked at the photos. There was one of the blond man standing in front of a house; in another he had his arm around a smiling woman who Mark guessed must be his wife. There were a lot of pictures of the two of them with a kid who looked about three years old.

"Our friend in Russia maybe will never see brother's wife, brother's son," said Olga. "It is important that we bring pictures." She returned the letter and photos to the envelope, rewrapped the watch, and returned both packets to the desk drawer.

"But why didn't Igor just explain?" asked Mark. "Dad would have understood. Is it against the rules for him to bring letters back? Would the other Russians have gotten him into trouble?"

Olga smiled, but it was a sad smile. "Rules . . . some rules we know, some we guess. Sometimes there can be trouble for little reason. For all physicists it is important to travel, and permission to travel is sometimes made difficult with very small reason, even without reason. In past, important all such things be secret. Secret means not telling even good friends, for if trouble comes, then maybe they will have trouble also because they help keep secret."

"That's why Igor didn't tell Misha and the others," said Mark slowly.

"Yes," agreed Olga. "You understand. Now things are changing, maybe already now brothers can send letters by mail and no trouble will come. Maybe no need for small mystery, maybe no need to protect friends. But we are not sure. Maybe also things can change back. So we try to keep secret."

"Then I shouldn't tell anyone about this?" asked Mark.

Olga thought. "If you wish, is okay to tell your father," she said. "He will know not to tell others. But please, do not tell children. Other children are not like you. They will not understand; they will make story each time more big, and maybe someone will hear who believes we do something bad, that we carry big secret, like spies. Someone in your government, our government."

Mark remembered how, not too many weeks ago, he himself had thought it would be exciting to prove that was just what they were doing! But the memory didn't embarrass him—it was as though that Mark were a lot younger, a different Mark. He felt as though he had grown up ten years in the last ten minutes.

For a fleeting instant, he thought how it was too bad he wouldn't be able to tell any of this to Jeff. It was more important than any of the stuff they did together. It made their talk about computer secrets seem like comic-book stuff. But he knew he was being trusted with a real secret. "It's okay," he said. "I won't tell anyone."

Olga gave his shoulder a hug and shook her head. "I hope that maybe in one, two years we can laugh that such ordinary thing must once be hidden. It is silly that we must play such game. I am sorry."

"It's okay," repeated Mark absently. He

was trying to imagine what the life Olga was going back to would be like. He wished now he had asked more questions about life in Russia—the difficult parts, the good parts. There wasn't time now, and, anyway, he wouldn't know where to begin. Nothing was simple.

The two of them returned to the task of laying out things for tea.

13

Mark's whole family went to the airport to see the Russians off. In addition to Igor Zhavoronkov and his family, the three other physicists Mark had gone shopping with were there. There was a lot of laughing and joking among the men as they all waited in line together to check their baggage. Mom chatted quietly with Olga, holding for Meg the box that Natasha had presented to her friend with instructions to open it after they had gone. The two little girls were silently holding hands, Natasha clutching close to her the new doll that was a going-away present from Mark's family.

Mark stood a little apart, wishing it were all over. He felt a little numb. This was like being at the dentist's: you knew you had to go through it, but it wasn't fun.

Before long, however, the baggage was checked in, and they were all approaching the final security check, beyond which only passengers could go. It was time for final farewells. Olga handed a tiny box to Mark's mother. "For you," she said. "I will always remember your family." The two women hugged.

There was a great flurry of handshaking and hugging. Each Russian physicist hugged Mark's father. His mother got a hug from Igor as well; the other men shook her hand. Meg started hugging everybody, even her own family. Natasha hugged Meg and Mark's mother and, after a moment of hesitation, Mark. Misha, Nicolai, and Sergei all shook Mark's hand, but Igor gave him a big bear hug.

Olga hugged all of Mark's family in turn,

coming to Mark last of all. She handed him a small package. "For you," she said, hugged him quickly, and was gone.

The family found a window overlooking the runway and waited there to see the big jet take off. It sped past, angled up, and disappeared into the sky.

As they drove home, Mark's mother took the wrappings off her little box. "Amber earrings!" she exclaimed. "How lovely! What's in your box, Meg?"

Meg untied the ribbon, took off the paper, and opened the box. Inside was a round, brightly painted wooden figure. "I don't know what it is," said Meg, puzzled.

Mom turned around to look. "Oh, it's one of those Russian dolls!" she said. "It comes apart, Meg, and there will be another little doll inside, and another one inside that, and so on. And then you can put all the halves together and you'll have lots of dolls."

Meg tried it, fitting each wooden doll back together as soon as she had taken out the smaller one inside. When she got to the last doll, a very tiny one, there was a little slip of paper around it. "What does it say?" she asked, handing it to Mark.

The writing was in uneven English letters. Mark could tell Natasha must have drawn the letters herself, although since she couldn't spell yet, someone else must have written the words out for her first. "It says, 'I will miss you.'"

"What's in your box?" asked Meg.

"I haven't opened it yet," said Mark.

"Well, open it!" demanded Meg.

"Twerp," said Mark, but he undid the ribbon, unwrapped the paper, and lifted the lid. Inside the box, in neat rows, were packed the same sort of Russian chocolates that Olga had served him on the afternoon of his first visit. "Candy," he announced. Then he noticed a piece of folded paper tucked inside the lid of the box. He unfolded it.

"What's that?" said Meg.

"A secret message," said Mark. He read it carefully, refolded the paper, and put it into his pocket.

"What did it say?" insisted Meg.

"If I told you, it wouldn't be a secret," said Mark. But then he looked down at his sister and saw that her eyes were pleading. He felt ashamed of himself. This was a kind of secret that could be shared. After all, he and Meg had shared those Wednesdays. Today couldn't be easy for her, either. He nudged her shoulder with his. "But maybe I might tell you after we get home if you don't make a pest of yourself on the way."

Meg nodded solemnly, satisfied, and started to put her nesting dolls inside one another again, her own private message safe back in the center with the tiniest doll. Mark leaned back in the seat and closed his eyes. He was beginning to feel better. The message inside his pocket was written in neat Russian capitals:

РИМЭМБЭР: АЙ ЭМ НАТ
ЛАЙК ВАСКА, АЙ ДУ НАТ
ФОРГЭТ Ю. МЭЙБИ ЮР
ФЭМЫЛИ ВЫЗЫЦ АС НЭКСТ?
СУН?

ОЛГА

Mark's Key to the Russian Alphabet

A = "ah" (father) or
    "uh" (ago)
Б = B
В = V
Г = g in get
Д = D
Е = "yeh" (yes)
Ё = "yo" (yoyo)
Ж = "zh" (treasure)
З = Z
И = "ee" (seen)
Й = Y
    АЙ = y in try
    ОЙ = oy in boy
    ЕЙ = ey in hey
К = K
Л = L
М = M

Н = N
О = o in open
П = P
Р = R
С = s in snow
Т = T
У = "oo" (boo)
Ф = F
Х = h in hat
Ц = "ts" (cats)
Ч = "ch" (chin)
Ш = "sh" (shin)
Щ = "sh"+"ch"
    (fresh cheese)
ы = i in sit
Э = e in set
Ю = "yoo" (use)
Я = "yah" (yacht)